Oh, My! Ginny Fry!

First Grade Trouble

by Gina Shaw
Illustrated by Patrice Barton

Scholastic Inc.
New York Toronto London Auckland Sydney
Mexico City New Delhi Hong Kong Buenos Aires

SO-AZX-683

To Jeff—
Thanks for listening and listening and listening . . .
and for your support always—G. S.

To a free-wheeling first grader, my son, Seth.
My inspiration then, my inspiration now—P. B.

No part of this publication may be reproduced, stored in a retrieval system, or transmitted in any form or by any means, electronic, mechanical, photocopying, recording, or otherwise, without written permission of the publisher. For information regarding permission, write to Scholastic Inc., Attention: Permissions Department, 557 Broadway, New York, NY 10012.

ISBN-13: 978-0-545-07079-9
ISBN-10: 0-545-07079-1

Text copyright © 2008 by Gina Shaw
Illustrations copyright © 2008 by Patrice Barton
All rights reserved. Published by Scholastic Inc.

SCHOLASTIC and associated logos are trademarks and/or registered trademarks of Scholastic Inc.

Lexile is a registered trademark of MetaMetrics, Inc.

12 11 10 9 8 7 6 5 4 3 2   8 9 10 11 12 13/0

Printed in the U.S.A.
First printing, October 2008

Book design by Jennifer Rinaldi Windau

Chapter 1

I like to run.

I like to jump.

I like to climb.

I like to sail paper airplanes

high in the sky.

But I can't do any of this today.

Today I have to go to school.

This morning after breakfast,

I told Mom, "I don't *always*

have to go to school."

Mom smiled her mom smile and

said, "Oh yes, you do."

So here I am sitting in the third

seat in the first row next to the

coat closet in Class 1-11.

BOR-ING!

I take out my crayon box

and pour my crayons

all over my desk.

The colors are very bright.

Mom bought me the Bright

and Bold box for school.

I pick up grass green.

I think of the park.

Lemon yellow is the sun.

Navy blue is the water in the lake.

Brick red is the boat I'm sitting in.

I'm rowing across the lake.

Faster, harder,

faster, harder.

I pass the sunset orange boat.

I pass the bark brown boat.

I pass the snow white boat.

I pass the purple pizzazz boat.

I make it to the other side—

in no time at all.

I'm the winner!

Yaay for me!

Chapter 2

"Regina, RE-GINA, **RE-GI-NA**,"

my teacher shouts.

She is standing over my desk.

I immediately leave the park

and the lake and my boat behind.

Am I in trouble? I wonder.

"Regina, I'm taking attendance,"

Ms. Hurley says. "Please answer

when you hear your name."

I look up at her.

I look up, up, up.

Ms. Hurley is very tall.

She's taller than Mom.

"Okay," I say. "I will answer when I hear my name."

I like this game.

"Regina," Ms. Hurley says again, looking straight at me.

I wonder.

I wonder why she keeps saying the word Regina.

I wait.

I wait until I hear my name.

Ms. Hurley waits.

I wait.

Silence.

Neither of us says a word.

Now this game is **BOR-ING**.

"RE-GI-NA!" Ms. Hurley yells

very loudly.

She glares at me.

"Why are you calling me that

name?" I ask. "My name is Ginny.

Everyone calls me Ginny.

Everyone except, of course, my

aunt, who calls me Gee-gee."

All the kids in my class think

this is funny.

Some giggle.

Some titter.

Some snigger.

Some chuckle.

And, one boy laughs very loudly.

Ms. Hurley does not giggle, titter, snigger, chuckle, or laugh loudly. Ms. Hurley just sighs.

"Regina is your real name," she says. "It's on your official school record. Ginny must be your nickname."

"But Ginny is what everyone calls me," I explain again. "Everyone except, of course, my aunt, who calls me Gee-gee."

"Mmm," Ms. Hurley says and lets out an even bigger sigh. "I guess we'll call you Ginny, too."

Yaay for me!

Chapter 3

Ms. Hurley walks to

the back of our classroom.

She is carrying a large,

colorful poster with a big wheel on it.

She hangs the poster on

the bulletin board.

We all turn around in our

chairs and watch her.

"Class," Ms. Hurley says, "this
is our job wheel. When I call out
a job that you'd like to have,
please raise your hand."
Everyone is excited.

"Okay, first job," Ms. Hurley says,

"is chalkboard monitor."

I raise my hand high.

Dustin and Jody raise their

hands, too.

"Ooh, pick me, pick me," I shout.

Ms. Hurley chooses Dustin.

He will erase the chalkboard

at the end of every day.

I sit back in my chair.

I sulk.

I feel bluer than my midnight

blue crayon.

"Next is paper monitor,"

announces Ms. Hurley.

I raise my hand higher than

I did before.

Alice raises her hand.

Bond raises his hand.

I stand on my chair and wave

my hand even higher.

Ms. Hurley picks Bond.

She doesn't even look at me.

Ms. Hurley calls out more jobs.

I raise my hand.

I shout, "Pick me. Pick me."

I stand on my chair.

I stand on my desk.

I jump up and down in the aisle.

But Ms. Hurley doesn't choose

me for any job.

Then Ms. Hurley says, "Last job—
who would like to be our bird
monitor? You will have to feed
Rocky every morning and make
sure he has water at the end
of the day."

I don't like birds.

I don't like their beaks.

I don't like their beady eyes.

I don't like their feathers.

And, I don't like the sound
their wings make when they fly.

Birds scare me – even if Rocky
is canary yellow.

I do like that color crayon.

I sit quietly at my desk.

I don't raise my hand.

I don't shout out.

I don't stand on my chair.

I don't stand on my desk.

I don't jump up and down

in the aisle.

"Ginny," Ms. Hurley says, "I see

you're behaving yourself now.

Since you don't have a job, you

can be our bird monitor."

"But, but, but," I start to say.

Too late!

Ms. Hurley has just written

my name on the job wheel.

I don't want to be the bird monitor.

Too bad for me!

Chapter 4

"Time to go outside," Ms. Hurley

announces, and she takes us to

the school playground.

I love to run. I love to jump.

I love to skip. I love to climb.

But today is not a good day.

I do not want to be

the bird monitor.

I sit down on the bench in the
schoolyard.

I put my head in my hands.

The boy who laughed the loudest
this morning sits down next to me.

He puts his head in his hands, too.

"What's your name?" I ask.

"Spike," he mutters.

"What kind of name is that?"
I ask.

"My name," he answers.

"Is it your real name? The one
that's on your official school
record?" I ask.

"No, but it's what everyone calls
me. Everyone except Ms. Hurley,"
he says. "She calls me Brian
because *that's* the name that's
on my official school record."
"So why did you tell me your
name is Spike?" I ask.

"You see," he explains. "I have a brother named Matt and a stepbrother named Matt.

One day my stepdad called a family meeting and said, 'We can't have two Matts in the same house. So I'm going to call out some nicknames. When you hear one you like, tell me. Okay, who wants the name Spike?'

I liked the name Spike so I shouted, 'I want it!'

I jumped up and down.

I stood on my chair.

I waved my arms in the air.

My stepdad said, 'Brian, you're
not the one who needs a
nickname! This meeting is over.'
My brothers laughed at me.
But I was happy.
I told my brothers, my mom, and
my stepdad that I wanted to be
called Spike from now on."
"Mmm," I say. "Can I call you
Spike, too?"
"Yup," he agrees.
"You're just like me!" I smile.
Yaay for us!

Chapter 5

Spike and I both put our
heads back in our hands.

"What's wrong with you?" I ask.

"This is a no-good, very bad day
for me," he says.

"For me too," I tell him. "Why is
it a bad day for you?"

"I don't want to be the plant

34

monitor," he says. "Plants make me sneeze. Plants make me wheeze. Plants don't do anything. Plants are **BOR-ING**."

I stand up tall on the bench.

I jump up and down.

I spring off it.

I shout, "Me too! Me too! I don't
want to be the bird monitor.
I don't like birds. I don't like their
beaks. I don't like their beady
eyes. I don't like their feathers.
And, I don't like the sound
their wings make when they fly.
Birds **scare** me."

We both put our heads back
in our hands.

Too bad for us.

Chapter 6

Suddenly, I look at Spike.

I grab his hand.

We jump off the bench together.

We fly into the school building.

We run into our classroom.

We race to my desk.

I pour my Bright and Bold

crayons all over it.

"Pick a color," I say.

Spike chooses neon carrot
orange.

I choose electric lime green.

I grab his hand again.

We dash to the job wheel

at the back of the room.

"Wait," Spike yells, "what are you doing? I don't want to get into trouble!"

"Don't worry," I tell him. "We won't get into trouble for *this*!"

I raise my electric lime crayon up to the job chart.

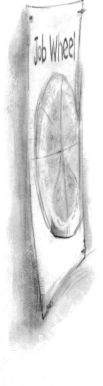

"Ginny, Brian, what are you doing?"

Ms. Hurley shouts as she walks

into the room.

Uh-oh.

We *are* in trouble.

Too bad for us.

Chapter 7

I start to speak very quickly.

This happens when I get nervous.

"You-see," I say to Ms. Hurley,

"Spike-and-I-don't-like-our-jobs.

We-want-to-switch-them-

and-I-was-going-to-change-our-

names-on-the—"

"*She* wanted to switch them,"

Spike interrupts and points at me.

"Whoa!" Ms. Hurley says. "Slow down! First of all, who is Spike?"

"I am," says Spike. "Brian is my name on my official school record. But everyone calls me Spike."

Ms. Hurley lets out a deep sigh.

"You, too?" she asks Spike. "You also want to be called by your nickname in our class?"

"Yes, please," says Spike.

Ms. Hurley doesn't say anything. Finally, she looks at me and asks, "What were you going to do to my job wheel?"

"We-were-going-to-switch-our-names-on-it. I-want-to-be-the-plant-monitor-and-Spike-will-take-care-of-Rocky. He-thinks-plants-are-boring-and-birds-

scare-me," I say, all in one breath.
"*She* was going to switch the

names on the job chart,"

Spike says again.

"Whoa, slow down," Ms. Hurley says. "Okay, first. Brian, I will call you Spike in our classroom from now on."

Spike smiles. I smile.

"Next," Ms. Hurley continues. "Spike, you can be the bird monitor. Ginny, you can be the plant monitor. But, next time, come to me first. Let's talk *before* you do something that might get you into trouble."

Ms. Hurley is the best teacher ever!

She even lets us change our
names on the job wheel.

Spike goes first.

He crosses out my name and
writes his with his neon carrot
orange crayon.

I do the same with my electric
lime green crayon.

We both thank Ms. Hurley.

Then we smile at each other.

This is going to be a good
school year.

Yaay for us!